Katie Fry
PRIVATE EYE

The Lost Kitten

Written by Katherine Cox
Illustrated by Vanessa Brantley Newton

D0028038

SCHOLASTIC INC.

ISBN 978-0-545-66672-5

Text copyright © 2015 by Katherine Cox
Illustrations copyright © 2015 by Vanessa Brantley Newton.
All rights reserved. Published by Scholastic Inc.
SCHOLASTIC and associated logos are trademarks and/or registered trademarks of Scholastic Inc.

12 11 10 9 8 7 6 5 4 3 2 1   15 16 17 18 19 20/0

Printed in the U.S.A.   40
First printing, February 2015

Designed by Maria Mercado

Chapter One

This is Katie.

"Pssst, down here!"

Katie is little, but has a big brain.

3

Katie loves to solve mysteries.
She solved the mystery of the lost glasses.

She solved the mystery of the missing cookie.

She even solved the mystery of the early bedtime.

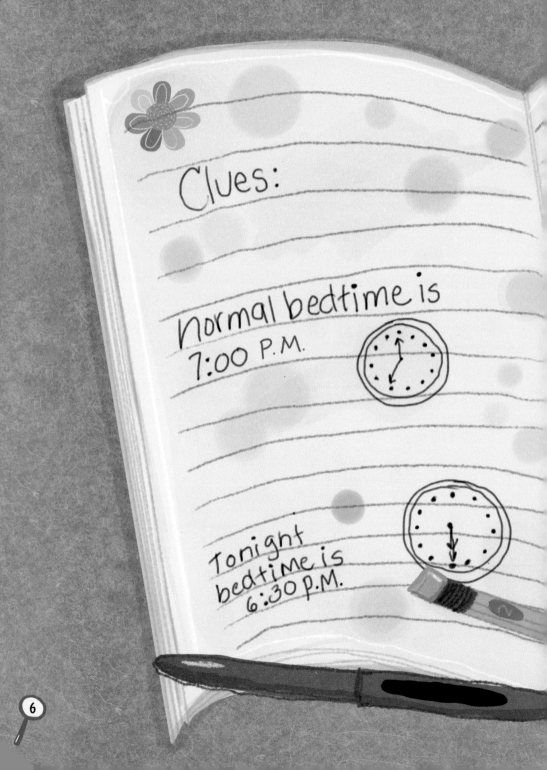

Clues:

normal bedtime is
7:00 P.M.

Tonight
bedtime is
6:30 P.M.

Mom and Dad
e dressed up

The kitchen
smells like
roast chicken

Someone lit
candles in the
dining room

Conclusion:
Parent date
night. YUCK!

Katie is looking for another mystery to solve.

Let Katie Solve
Your Mysteries!

Free!
(No Refunds)

"I saw a kitten alone in the park..."
says Mailman Bob.

Katie knows what to do.

Chapter Two

This is Sherlock.

"Pssst, over here!"

WELCOME TO THE PARK!
Perfect for Adventures!

Sherlock likes to explore.

"Do you need some help?" Katie asks Sherlock.
Sherlock looks this way and that way.
He looks up and down and all around.

"I am just a little lost," he says.

It's the mystery of the lost kitten!
Katie says, "I'll take the case."

"What case?" Sherlock asks.
"Trust me," says Katie. "I know what to do."

Chapter Three

Katie writes down the clues.

Someone has trimmed the kitten's nails.

His coat is brushed and cared for.

The fur around his neck is pushed down.

"Someone has been taking care of you,"
says Katie. "Looks like you once had a home...
and a collar."

"If only we could find it," says Sherlock.
That gives Katie an idea!

"We need to find anyone who saw you wearing that collar," says Katie.

Sherlock asks, "Like witnesses?"
"I like the way you think," says Katie.

Do you know this cat? Talk to Katie!

Chapter Four

Soon, it is time for lunch.
Katie asks Sherlock if he is hungry.

"We have tuna fish," she says.
"You had me at lunch," says Sherlock.

As they eat, Katie asks Sherlock to tell her everything he noticed that morning. "Blue sky, hard stones, yellow feathers, and tall trees," says Sherlock.

Katie hears a peck on the window.
"Those are the yellow feathers!" says Sherlock.

WELCOME TO THE PARK!
Perfect for Adventures!

"I saw the kitten lose his collar," the bird on the windowsill tells them.
"Where?" asks Katie.
"Look for a pile of stones," says the bird.

Sherlock looks confused.
But the bird has no time for more questions.
He has to fly.

"A pile of stones..."
Katie has that look on her face. The one that means her big brain is hard at work.

Sherlock follows her back to the park.
He doesn't know why.

"We solved the mystery," Katie says.
"And now we know where you live."
But Katie doesn't want to say good-bye.

"Maybe I could get lost in the park again," Sherlock suggests.
"I have an even better idea," Katie says.

Let Katie Solve Your Mysteries!

Free! (No Refunds)

Let Katie (and Sherlock) Solve Your Mysteries!

Free!
(No Refunds)